WORLD WAR II
NIGHT BEFORE CHRISTMAS

For Marie and Melanie

Published by Magnum Books
Maple Grove, MN
www.mikeguardia.com
Copyright © 2018 by Mike Guardia
All Rights Reserved
Illustrations and Cover courtesy of Melanie Stephens
www.MSIllustrations.com
First published 2018
Manufactured in the United States
Guardia, Mike.
World War II Night Before Christmas
Mike Guardia
ISBN: 978-0-9996443-9-3

WORLD WAR II
NIGHT BEFORE CHRISTMAS

By Mike Guardia
Illustrated By Melanie Stephens

Magnum Books

T'WAS THE NIGHT BEFORE CHRISTMAS,
when along the frontlines...

The whole U.S. Army
was in a race against time.

The GIs dug foxholes
in the forests with care,
In hopes that the Nazis
soon would be there.

Together we huddled,
with feelings of dread.
While visions of D-Day
replayed in my head.

On this night before Christmas, 1944
Not a trooper was happy to be fighting this war...

But the world was in trouble
And we answered the call,
To get rid of the Nazis once and for all.

It was freezing that night,
nearly fifteen below,
With nothin' to protect us
from the wind and the snow.

But Joe with his mortar,
And me with my gun,
Stood ready to fight
'til this battle was won.

When out from the woods
there arose such a clatter
I sprang to my feet to see what
was the matter.

I steadied my rifle,
my hands on the trigger...
As that sound in the woods
grew bigger and bigger.

That rumbling sound then grew to a roar
And I yelled:

When what to my wandering eyes should appear
But a miniature sled and eight tiny reindeer
"Hold your fire!" I yelled,
For I had reason to pause.

"Joe, am I going crazy… or is that Santa Claus?"

Yes ol' St. Nick himself was perched on that seat,
With a cigar in his teeth and jump boots on his feet
A steel-pot helmet sat snug on his head
And fatigues had replaced his bright suit of red.

The rank of a General sat high on his collar,
And with a cup of his hand, gave the reindeer a holler :
"Now Dasher, Now Dancer, Now Prancer, Now Vixen,
On Comet, On Cupid, On Donner, and Blizten!"

Louder than Panzers,
his coursers they came,
And halted the sled as he
pulled up the reins.

He flung from his shoulder
a green duffle bag,
And approached our position
with a true GI swag.
From his boots to his brow,
he was a soldier's sensation,
Though his belly and beard
were beyond regulation.

He said not a word,
but went straight on his way
to fill up our foxholes with
goods from his sleigh.

There were jackets and
blankets and warm winter clothes,
and new leather boots for our frostbitten toes.

There were sleeping bags, coffee,
and rations brand new.
"Merry Christmas," he said,
"To the Red, White, and Blue!"

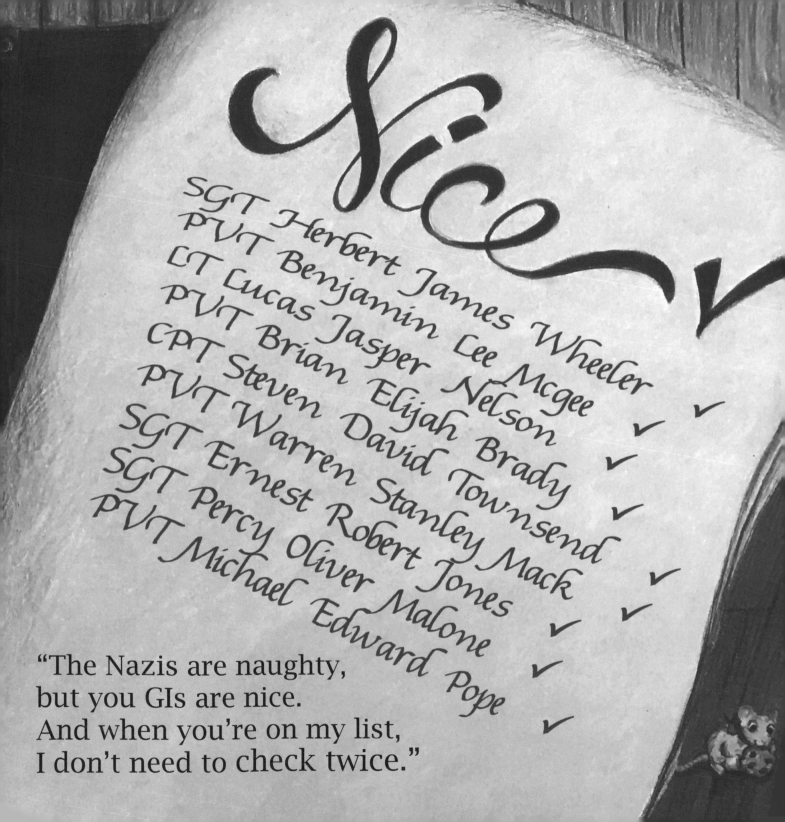

Nice

SGT Herbert James Wheeler
PVT Benjamin Lee Mcgee
LT Lucas Jasper Nelson ✓
PVT Brian Elijah Brady ✓
CPT Steven David Townsend ✓
PVT Warren Stanley Mack ✓
SGT Ernest Robert Jones ✓
SGT Percy Oliver Malone ✓
PVT Michael Edward Pope ✓

"The Nazis are naughty,
but you GIs are nice.
And when you're on my list,
I don't need to check twice."

But 'ol Father Christmas kept his yuletide composure,
And with a wink of his eye, placed his hand on my shoulder.
"Rest easy, Sergeant," he said, "I've accomplished my mission,
To bring holiday cheer to this combat division.

See, I know the difference 'tween
what's wrong and what's right,
And I reward those who fight the good fight."

With that, he turned and shuffled
back towards his sleigh,
Stowed his green duffle,
and was soon on his way.
But I did hear him holler,
as he rode out of sight:

"MERRY CHRISTMAS, MY TROOPS...
AND TO ALL A GOOD NIGHT!"

About the Author

Mike Guardia is an award-winning author, historian, and the father of two wonderful girls. *World War II Night Before Christmas* is his second children's book.

CPSIA information can be obtained
at www.ICGtesting.com
Printed in the USA
LVHW050133091219
639846LV00002B/53/P